Brian John has had a varied career as an Arctic and Antarctic explorer, geography lecturer, environmental activist, and writer. *House of Angels* is the sequel to his first novel, *On Angel Mountain*, which is also published by Corgi Books.

# HOUSE OF ANGELS

## Brian John

CORGI BOOKS

**HOUSE OF ANGELS**
**A CORGI BOOK : 0552153281**
**9780552153287**

Originally published in Great Britain by Greencroft Books

PRINTING HISTORY
Greencroft Books edition published 2002
Corgi edition published 2006

1 3 5 7 9 10 8 6 4 2

Set in 11/13 pt Palatino by
Falcon Oast Graphic Art Ltd.

Corgi Books are published by Transworld Publishers,
61–63 Uxbridge Road, London W5 5SA,
a division of The Random House Group Ltd,
in Australia by Random House Australia (Pty) Ltd,
20 Alfred Street, Milsons Point, Sydney, NSW 2061, Australia,
in New Zealand by Random House New Zealand Ltd,
18 Poland Road, Glenfield, Auckland 10, New Zealand,
in South Africa by Random House (Pty) Ltd, Isle of Houghton,
Corner of Boundary Road & Carse O'Gowrie, Houghton 2198, South Africa,
and in India by Random House Publishers India Private Limited,
301 World Trade Tower, Hotel Intercontinental Grand Complex,
Barakhamba Lane, New Delhi 110 001, India.

Printed and bound in Great Britain by
Cox & Wyman Ltd, Reading, Berkshire.

Papers used by Transworld Publishers are natural, recyclable
products made from wood grown in sustainable forests. The
manufacturing processes conform to the environmental
regulations of the country of origin.

To Inger
and all those who love
*Angel Mountain*

# Acknowledgements

First and foremost, I thank my wife Inger for her endless help and encouragement in the writing of my first work of fiction, *On Angel Mountain*, and now this sequel. She realized better than I what pleasure was to be gained from the creative process, and from the discovery that my characters and my fantasy world could give pleasure to others. She has acted as in-house editorial adviser, reviewer and proof-reader, and without her personal and professional input, the finished products would have looked very unpolished! Stephen, Alison and Martin, Heather and Ken, Hilary and Richard have all given huge support, as have many other relatives and friends. I thank them all. Those who have read and commented kindly on the first story about Martha Morgan have also spurred me on to the completion of this sequel, and I hope that I have been able to meet their high expectations.

A great deal of research has gone into *House of Angels*, and I should like to acknowledge my debt to various publications by Richard Rose, Robert Hughes, David

Howell, Dillwyn Miles, Trefor Owen, Fred Archer, Iorwerth Peate, Pat Molloy, Alexander Cordell, Francis Jones and William Cobbett. Two other books have been invaluable in helping me to capture 'the mood of the times' – Jane Austen's *Pride and Prejudice* and Anne Hughes's *Diary of a Farmer's Wife*. Many people have provided me with technical information relating to parts of the story, and I thank them all.

I am grateful to Irene Payne, Ian Richardson, Rowena Lord and my wife Inger for refereeing and commenting upon earlier versions of the text. Finally, a word of appreciation to the Welsh Books Council. The practical support of staff has been invaluable, and I acknowledge in particular the reader's report on a draft of *On Angel Mountain* which encouraged me to believe that I had something to say, and that there was somebody out there who might be willing to join me in my fantasy world.

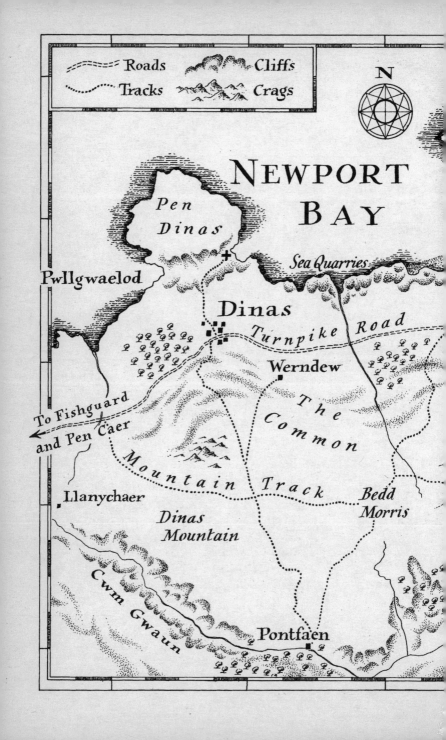

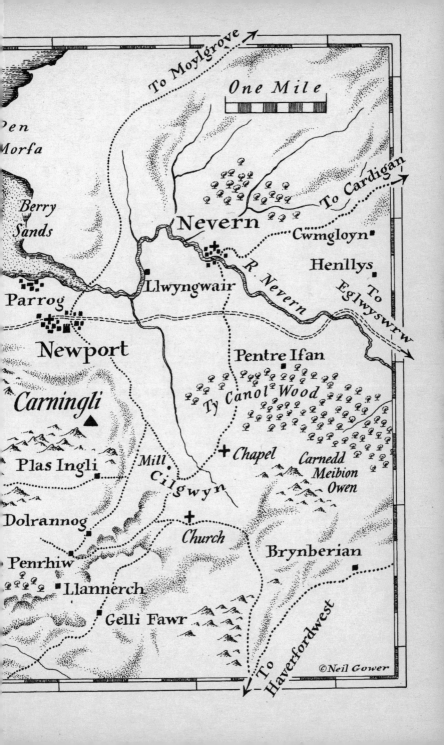

THE MORGAN FAMILY OF PLAS INGLI

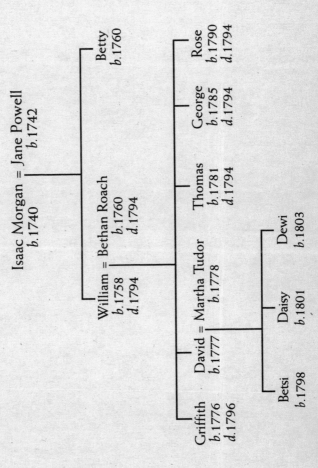

Isaac Morgan = Jane Powell
b.1740           b.1742

William = Bethan Roach          Betty
b.1758    b.1760                 b.1760
d.1794    d.1794

Griffith    David = Martha Tudor    Thomas      George      Rose
b.1776     b.1777    b.1778         b.1781      b.1785      b.1790
d.1796                              d.1794      d.1794      d.1794

Betsi       Daisy       Dewi
b.1798      b.1801      b.1803

b. = birth date
d. = death date